THE CAT AND THE MOON

33 Zen Stories to Slow Down, Calm the Mind, Relieve
Stress, and Find Peace Now

Zen Tales

Book 1

KAI TSUKIMI

Dedicated to Kat

A Free Gift For Readers 🌿

A book can shift your perspective, but a ritual can transform your life. As a thank-you for reading, I'd like to offer you our exclusive *Zen Clarity Kit*, designed to help you clear your mind, refocus, and make Zen teachings a part of your daily routine.

What's Inside the Kit?

✔ **The Zen Morning Ritual Guide** – A simple daily practice to anchor your mind in stillness.

✔ **A 5-Minute Audio Meditation** – Gently guide yourself into a state of clarity and focus.

✔ **Zen Minimalism Wallpapers** – Subtle reminders to cultivate presence throughout your day.

>> Scan the QR Code or click here
to download your free gift <<

Table of Contents

Part IV

Moonlight Without Shape

Introduction

What Is Zen?

If you ask ten Zen masters what Zen is, you'll get ten different answers—and all of them will be true, and none of them will be complete.

Some will tell you it's the art of living in the present moment.

Some will say it's the sound of one hand clapping.

Others might stare at you in silence, or laugh, or hand you a cup of tea.

The trouble is, the more you try to define Zen, the further it slips away. It doesn't live in definitions. It lives in direct experience—in the moments you weren't expecting, when life catches you off guard, and you suddenly realize you were holding the answer all along.

And in this book, it lives in the shape of a cat.

Why a Cat?

Because if Zen were to take form, it might very well show up as a cat—appearing when it pleases, ignoring you when you try too hard, curling up in the most inconvenient places, and slipping away just when you think you've finally figured it out.

A cat does not explain itself. It does not wait for permission. It does not care whether you approve.

And yet, when it chooses to sit quietly beside you under the moonlight, you feel something shift—something that can't quite be named. You realize you've been chasing your own tail all along, when everything you were looking for was already here, breathing in rhythm with the night.

The moon, of course, has always been part of the story. In Zen, the moon often represents truth—unreachable, yet reflected in every puddle, every bowl of tea, every pair of eyes that dares to stop and look. We chase it, we grasp at its reflection, but we can never quite catch it. Because the truth isn't something you catch. It's something you notice when you stop trying.

What Are Zen Stories?

Zen stories are not lessons in the traditional sense. They don't give you answers, and they aren't interested in helping you "improve." In fact, they often do the opposite. They throw you off balance, challenge what you think you know, and leave you standing in the middle of your life wondering how you didn't see it sooner.

Some Zen stories are absurd.

Some are poetic.

Some are downright frustrating.

But all of them share one thing: they point you back to what's real—not by explaining it, but by helping you experience it for yourself.

This book is a collection of 33 Zen stories, all following the quiet wanderings of a cat beneath the light of the moon. The stories are strange, sometimes humorous, sometimes haunting, and occasionally disorienting. They are not meant to be solved. They are meant to be felt.

How to Use This Book

You won't find any steps to follow here. No seven-day plans. No promises of enlightenment. Just stories.

You can read them all at once or one at a time. You can open the book to any page and start there. Or you can let the cat lead you—read slowly, let the words settle like ripples on still water, and notice what catches you by surprise.

At the end of each part, you'll find an optional invitation to dive deeper into the stories. These are not explanations or lessons—just simple nudges toward reflection. You might find that these questions awaken something in you. Or you might feel nothing at all. Both are perfectly fine. Zen doesn't require understanding. It only asks that you show up, just as you are.

So pour yourself some tea.

Find a quiet place to sit.

And let the cat and the moon show you what can't be put into words.

Because the truth you've been looking for isn't waiting at the end of the path.

It's already here, in the space you're standing in right now.

You just have to notice.

— *Kai*

PART I
Mist & Whiskers

IF YOU ARE UNABLE TO FIND THE TRUTH
RIGHT WHERE YOU ARE, WHERE ELSE DO
YOU EXPECT TO FIND IT?

Dōgen Zenji

1

THE CAT WHO THOUGHT IT WAS A MONK

THE CAT ARRIVED ON A TUESDAY. OR PERHAPS it had always been there.

No one had seen it enter the temple. Yet the incense curled in wild loops that morning, and the rice pot boiled over without sound. The leaves in the courtyard stirred, though the air was still.

That was the cat's way.

It spent three days on the roof beam, peering down at the monks like a tiny emperor surveying his court. It blinked when they bowed. Tilted its head during their chants. Swiped lazily at a spider as they sat in stillness.

But on the fourth morning, it descended.

Without announcement or hesitation, the cat took its place on an empty cushion beside the master. Its posture was near perfect—tail curled precisely, paws tucked like a statue of Manjushri. Its green eyes, half-lidded, reflected the faint shimmer of the morning bell. When the bell rang, the cat did not flinch.

The monks glanced at one another, but no one dared disturb it. It sat more still than some of the novices.

That evening, as they rose to chant, the cat rose too. It lifted one paw, placing it awkwardly on the floor as if bowing. Then, it opened its mouth and released a long, wailing meow—off-key, unhurried, echoing through the zendo like some ancient spirit clearing its throat.

The monks bit their tongues to keep from laughing. But the cat, emboldened, continued. It followed the rhythm of the chant with rising and falling meows, slightly out of time but strangely earnest. It swayed side to side, bumping into a young monk's knee. The monk shifted, trying to ignore it, but the cat fixed him with a look as if daring him to break the ritual.

And then, in one audacious leap, the cat pounced onto the master's own cushion, kneaded it with relentless devotion, and settled in—tail flicking like a metronome.

Muffled laughter stirred.

Later, in the refectory, a novice whispered, "Master, is it mocking us or teaching us?"

Master Dōken sipped his tea, letting the question hang like mist.

The cat returned the next day, and the next. It copied everything. When the monks bowed, it flopped sideways in a crooked, awkward heap. When they swept the court-yard, it chased the broom bristles like a kitten possessed.

During prostrations, it rolled onto its back and stretched all four legs toward the ceiling, paws trembling in some feline gesture of surrender. One monk swore he saw it squint one eye, as if testing who dared to break their composure first.

Soon, some monks began to avoid the zendo altogether, muttering about distractions and mockery. Others watched in quiet wonder, uncertain whether they were witnessing nonsense or a mystery deeper than their own efforts.

One night, as the moon climbed full and bright, the chanting began again. The cat stood, stretched in exaggerated silence, and walked to the center of the hall.

The monks froze as the cat slowly turned to face them all.

Then, without warning, Master Dōken stood, bent down on all fours, and began to crawl after the cat—moving with unsettling precision, shoulder blades rising like small mountains beneath his robe.

The monks watched, eyes wide, until one—then another—followed, some crawling, some bowing, some laughing softly without knowing why.

Out through the temple door they went—like a strange, crawling river—across the stone courtyard, past the garden lanterns, into the open field beyond.

The cat trotted ahead, tail high, leading them in wide, meandering circles beneath the silver light.

At last, it paused beneath an old cedar, yawned, and curled into a tight ball, ignoring them entirely.

The monks stood in the grass, bewildered. Some sat. Some remained on all fours. No one spoke.

The wind shifted. A cloud passed over the moon. Somewhere, a night bird called.

And then, with no ceremony at all, the cat stood, walked back to the zendo, and claimed the master's cushion once again—sitting tall, eyes fixed on the great bell hanging in the corner.

Master Dōken stood behind it, watching the monks shuffle back in. He leaned down toward the cat, so softly that only the nearest could hear.

"Who's the monk now?"

The bell remained silent. The cat did not move.

And that was the end of it.

But from that night on, the cat was never given just a cushion. It was given *the* cushion.

And no one, not once, dared to sit there again.

2

THE BOWL OF SKY

It was a ceramic bowl, chipped at the rim and glazed the color of morning.

Someone had left it in the courtyard. Maybe by accident. Maybe not.

The cat found it just after dawn.

Inside the bowl: the sky.

Pale blue, cloud-flecked, and still.

The cat crouched low, eyes wide. Its whiskers trembled with wonder.

It sniffed the bowl, circled it twice, and then—delicately —tried to drink.

Nothing.

It pawed the edge. The sky rippled.

A small cloud wobbled.

The cat tried again, licking carefully, but its tongue met only dust and porcelain.

Across the courtyard, a young girl sweeping the temple steps noticed.

She tiptoed over. "What are you doing?" she whispered.

The cat didn't answer, of course.

She leaned in, peered into the bowl—and gasped.

The sky stared back.

"It's holding the sky," she said.

The cat blinked.

The girl ran to fetch the others. Monks, children, the cook with flour still on his hands. They gathered around, gazing into the bowl. Some saw sky. Others saw nothing. One swore he saw stars, even though it was morning.

Someone whispered, "Is it magic?"

"No," said the cook. "It's just water."

"But there's no water," said another.

Master Dōken stepped forward. He looked into the bowl, then at the cat. Then at the sky.

He picked up the bowl, turned it slowly, and tilted it just so—until the sky slipped out, vanishing with the angle.

"Ah," he said softly. "Empty again."

He set the bowl down and walked away.

One by one, the others left too, murmuring and shrugging.

But the cat stayed. And when everyone was gone, it sat beside the bowl, watching it fill again with the sky.

This time, it didn't try to drink.

3

THE BIRD WHO KNEW THE CAT'S NAME

THE CAT WAS NAPPING ON A TEMPLE WALL, ONE paw dangling lazily in the sun, when the bird arrived.

It wasn't a quiet bird.

It wasn't a polite one either.

It landed with a squawk so sharp it shook a cherry blossom loose.

"*Akira!*" it shouted.

The cat's ear twitched.

"*Akira!*" the bird cried again, hopping closer. "Isn't that your name?"

The cat opened one eye.

It did not recognize the name.

But the eye blinked once. Slowly.

"Thought so," the bird said, puffing its feathers proudly. "Names stick to creatures like leaves stick to wind."

The cat stood up and stretched. It circled once, then twice.

And lay down again.

"You're ignoring me," the bird observed.

The cat said nothing.

"Well, I suppose it doesn't matter," the bird went on. "Everyone has a name. Yours is just the kind that purrs when you forget it."

The cat yawned.

"Would you like to know mine?" asked the bird, tilting its head.

The cat stared.

The bird ruffled its wings. "No? Fair enough."

It hopped once, then flew up, circling the temple roof.

Just as it vanished beyond the eaves, it cawed:

"*Akira!*"

The cat watched the sky long after the bird was gone.

Then it turned, walked to the garden gate, and paused beside a stone.

Scratched faintly on its surface was a word the cat couldn't read.

But for some reason, it stayed there a long time.

4

THE MASTER WHO BARKED

THE TEMPLE HAD ALWAYS HUMMED WITH familiar sounds—the murmur of water in the garden basin, the rustling of robes as monks crossed the courtyard, the steady tap of the old broom sweeping fallen petals.

Even the temple cat played its part, filling the halls with purrs and meows.

But lately, something had shifted.

It began subtly enough. During the morning chants, the master—revered for his perfect timing and unwavering tone—began to hum.

Not softly, nor sweetly, but off-key. A lopsided melody that tangled with the harmony like a thread pulled loose from a monk's robe. The first time it happened, the monks glanced up like startled birds. When it happened again, they avoided each other's eyes.

Later, in the shoe hall, the master left his sandals upside down—soles facing the sky like small boats overturned in the tide. One monk paused, bent to right them, then hesitated.

He straightened up and left them as they were. Another monk whispered, "Is he... slipping?" A third nodded gravely. They carried these whispers with the same reverence they gave the old sutras, as if even confusion deserved a place on the altar.

The cat, too, had noticed. It began to paw at the upturned sandals. More than once, it was caught mimicking the master's off-key hum, a low, throaty sound vibrating in its chest, tail curling like a question mark.

And so the unease spread, soft as smoke, filling the spaces between breath and bow.

One dawn, the meditation bell rang.

The monks filed into the hall. The cat took its usual place by the door, tail flicking in a slow rhythm.

Silence grew dense, as if the air itself had thickened. Breath. Stillness. The long, unbroken hum of presence.

Then, from the front of the room, the master barked.

Not a single sharp bark, but a sequence—low, rhythmic, deliberate. Like the call of some temple dog. One bark. Two. Three. Then a pause. Another two, softer, almost playful.

The monks froze, their spines turning to bamboo. Some clenched their jaws. Some pressed their hands tighter to their laps. One swallowed so hard it echoed like thunder in his own ears.

Still the master barked, head slightly tilted, as if answering some unseen companion just outside the walls. The sound was not frantic or mad, but alive—so alive it unsettled the very notion of "right practice."

And then—he stopped.

Only the echo remained, folding itself into the silence.

The master turned to face the assembly, the corners of his mouth curled—not in mockery, but in something deeper. Mischief? Compassion? Who could say?

At that moment, the cat, who had been stone-still, let out a single, raspy meow. Not its usual whisper of sound, but something... different. Something that startled the monks more than all the barking had. It cracked the tension like dry wood in a winter fire.

A ripple of laughter rose—first hesitant, then helpless, spilling through the hall. Some monks leaned on each other, others wiped tears from their eyes. One slapped the floor, laughing so hard his face turned red.

The master simply bowed once, slow and deep, as if bowing to the laughter itself, then walked out without a word.

The monks, still catching their breath, slowly unfolded

their legs. A few glanced toward the cat, which sat serenely, licking its paw as if nothing at all had happened.

And yet something had.

From that day on, the cat would occasionally let out a single, strange yowl—a sound not quite a meow, not quite a bark—at the most unexpected moments: in the middle of silent meals, during the solemn ringing of the bell, or just as someone reached for their sandals.

And every time, the monks would find themselves teetering at the edge of laughter or wonder, never quite sure which. The sound left them lighter, yet unsettled— like standing on the edge of a great, invisible joke whose punchline would never fully arrive.

And so the temple returned to its quiet rhythm, now laced with the softest trace of absurdity.

The sandals still lay upside down.

The cat still watched and listened.

And the master?

He never barked again.

But sometimes—just sometimes—his lips moved as if he might.

5

THE SANDAL BY THE DOOR

THE MONK PLACED HIS SANDALS BY THE DOOR each night—side by side, heel to heel.

And each morning, one was missing.

Never both.

Never neither.

Always one.

At first, he smiled.

A small game, he thought.

Nothing more.

But after a week, the small game began to gnaw at him.

He rose earlier.

He waited by the door.

He watched the shadows shift in the garden, his breath growing tight in his chest.

One morning, just before the sky began to pale,

he saw it—a flick of a tail and a quiet shape slipping through the reeds.

The cat.

He reached for his sandals, ready to chase it down—to put an end to whatever this was.

But his hand stopped halfway.

He looked down at the single sandal.

Then at his bare foot pressed against the cold floor.

He stayed there a long moment, longer than he meant to.

And then, he left the sandal where it was.

Stepped out barefoot, feeling the sharp stones beneath him, the roughness of the path, the cool breath of the earth curling around his toes.

He walked like that all day, something in him loosening with every step.

The next morning, both sandals were gone.

And for the first time, his feet felt like they belonged to the ground.

6

THE MIRROR WITH NO REFLECTION

THEY SAID THE MIRROR HAD NO REFLECTION.

The cat found it by accident—in a small back room behind a door that hadn't slid open in years.

The air inside smelled of cedar and old paper.

Moonlight spilled through the torn shoji, falling in a thin line across the floor, ending at the mirror.

It was perfectly round. Perfectly still.

The cat approached slowly, its body low, whiskers trembling at something it couldn't name.

It looked inside.

No cat.

No room.

No moon.

Only silver.

Endless, soft, unmoving silver.

The cat lifted a paw, half-expecting to see it rise in return.

But nothing moved.

It leaned closer, pressing its nose toward the glass, half-hoping to fog it with breath—to prove something was there.

The glass stayed clear.

The cat's tail twitched, a small pulse of unease spreading through its chest.

It turned to leave, but froze when it heard the soft scrape of footsteps behind it.

The old master entered without a word.

He stood beside the cat, both of them staring into the same silent nothing.

After a long breath, the master spoke, barely above a whisper.

"There was a time I used to see myself here," he said.

The cat didn't move.

The master leaned in slightly, his voice heavier now.

"But one night...I saw someone else."

His face shifted, as if remembering something that had never fully left.

"She smiled at me," he whispered.

"A face I didn't know. And when I blinked...the mirror was empty."

He turned toward the door, but paused with his hand resting on the frame.

"If you ever see the cat here," he said softly, "tell it... I never stopped watching."

And then he was gone.

The cat stared at the glass a little longer, its breath shallow, its body still.

It didn't know if it had come closer to something, or if it had slipped further away.

But when it turned to leave, it did not look back.

And in the silence that followed, the mirror seemed to shimmer,

just once—as if remembering something neither of them could see.

7

THE CAT WHO SAT IN A CIRCLE

IT BEGAN, AS THESE THINGS OFTEN DO, WITH A simple line no one thought much about.

The children were playing in the temple courtyard, dragging pieces of chalk across the stones, drawing dragons, birds, and crooked hopscotch squares.

When the cat passed by, one of them knelt down and carefully drew a circle around it—not touching its fur, not too tight, just wide enough to leave space.

"There," she whispered.

"Now it can't leave."

The others gathered close, watching with wide, expectant eyes.

The cat blinked, glanced down at the pale white line, then back up at the faces leaning over it.

It didn't move.

Minutes passed.

The children waited.

The cat shifted its paws slightly, leaned forward, but stopped just before the edge.

It stretched its neck as if testing the air beyond the line, ears twitching at something no one else could hear.

And then, without warning, it sat down—tail curled close, body still,

eyes steady.

The children whispered again, a little more uncertain this time.

Some laughed.

Some lost interest.

One by one, they drifted away.

But the cat remained.

It watched the wind move through the garden.

Watched the light shift on the stones.

Watched the chalk begin to blur and fade.

A monk passed by and paused, watching from a distance without interrupting.

"Is it trapped?" a novice asked softly behind him.

The monk didn't answer right away.

"It hasn't tried to leave," he finally replied, his voice quieter than the breeze.

The cat stood slowly, eyes never leaving the edge of the circle.

It lifted one paw, held it in the air just long enough to feel the weight of the decision, then placed it down *inside* the line.

It walked once around the circle, then again, each step slow and deliberate, tracing the boundary as if memorizing something only it could understand.

On the third lap, it paused.

Turned to face outward, tail toward the center, eyes fixed on the world beyond the line.

And it sat.

As if leaving or staying had never really been the question at all.

8

THE FISH WHO REFUSED ENLIGHTENMENT

THE CAT HAD BEEN WATCHING THE POND FOR an hour.

The surface shimmered under the early morning sun. Beneath the lily pads, koi swam in lazy loops—orange, white, black, and gold, like molten jewels adrift in a quiet sky.

The temple cat's purrs and meows, soft as breath through a flute, usually filled the air as it watched the koi below. But this morning, there was only stillness. Only the hunt.

One fish—fat, slow, suspiciously self-important—glided just beneath the surface, moving as if it owned the pond. The cat tracked it, eyes narrowing, tail twitching in slow, mechanical intervals.

Paw lifted.

Held.

Held...

Then—

Splash!

The paw sliced the water with the elegance of a falling brick. The fish darted aside with all the effort it had.

It surfaced, calm as stone, and stared directly at the dripping cat.

The cat, wide-eyed and soaked to the whiskers, stiffened as the fish spoke—its voice strangely deep, almost theatrical.

"Ah, seeker of fleeting truths," the fish intoned, swiveling slowly to face the cat head-on. "Do you come again, like all who thirst for wisdom, only to muddy the waters with your trembling paw?"

The cat blinked once. Twice.

The fish floated closer, raising a single fin dramatically.

"I know what you seek," it continued, pausing for effect. "You think I am a symbol... a shimmering metaphor... the golden gate to enlightenment itself."

The cat leaned lower, muscles tense.

"But I refuse!" the fish declared, slapping its tail on the surface with the flair of a street performer. "Do you hear me? I refuse enlightenment! Too slippery for my fins, too drafty for my scales! I'd rather nibble algae than nibble at Nirvana!"

The cat's ear twitched.

"You monks and your questions," the fish sneered, circling with exaggerated loops. "What is the sound of one fin flapping? What is the color of no color? What nonsense! I would rather debate the virtues of pond scum!"

The cat, losing its composure, swatted the water again —missed—and in frustration, began chasing its own tail, spinning in a ridiculous whirl, eyes wide with disbelief.

The monks seated nearby noticed the ruckus.

"Did you hear that?" one whispered.

"I think the fish is... teaching," another replied gravely.

A third stroked his chin. "Perhaps it's testing our grasp of non-attachment."

Meanwhile, the fish wasn't done.

It lifted itself half out of the water, balancing awkwardly on its tail, like some bloated aquatic sage addressing an invisible audience.

"I am the unsolvable riddle! The unpluckable fruit! The untasted soup!" it roared. "And if this temple dares call me a lesson, let the lesson be this—let me be free of your meanings!"

With that, the fish flipped into the air with a flamboyant twist, spraying the cat from head to tail. It left behind a single, glistening bubble—rising, rising...

Pop.

Right on the cat's nose.

Soaked, dripping, eyes wide with what could only be described as existential defeat, the cat sat frozen on the stone edge of the pond.

The monks watched in reverent silence.

Finally, one leaned toward the others and whispered,

"Maybe... the fish is the master."

No one laughed.

No one spoke.

The cat licked its paw—once, slowly—as though it had never understood anything less... or more.

And somewhere, beneath the lily pads, the fish swam in slow, absurd circles, entirely, gloriously uncatchable.

Reflection Questions

FOR BEGINNERS

What in your life feels quietly alive, yet easy to overlook?

When was the last time you noticed something that
didn't ask to be explained?

How do you tend to respond when something familiar
begins to feel unfamiliar?

How do you tend to fill empty spaces—and what
happens if you don't?

PART II
Reflections in the Fur

HAPPINESS IS THE ABSENCE OF THE
STRIVING FOR HAPPINESS.

Chuang Tzu

9

THE CAT WHO FORGOT THE WAY BACK

THE CAT LEFT WITHOUT MEANING TO.

It had followed a scent—sweet and unfamiliar—beyond the temple garden, past the stone path, into the dry grass where the wind moved like breath without a body.

By the time the scent disappeared, the cat had gone too far to recognize anything.

The trees were taller here.

The air heavier.

The light bent at odd angles, like the day wasn't sure how to hold itself.

The cat circled once. Then twice.

It pawed the dirt. Meowed quietly. Listened.

No sound came back.

It tried to retrace its steps, but there were no steps to follow.

No scratch marks on bark. No worn stones. No thread of scent leading home.

The cat sat.

Not because it understood. Just because it didn't know what else to do.

Time passed the way fog moves across water—without shape, without hurry.

At some point, a bird landed nearby. It did not speak. It only looked at the cat and tilted its head, as if it too had once gone too far.

The cat blinked. Closed its eyes.

Then opened them again.

There was a path now.

Not one the cat remembered walking. Not one it had seen before. But it was there. Curved. Dappled in shadow. Leading *somewhere*.

The cat stood, stretched, and walked it—without knowing where it led.

And without needing to.

10

THE NAME BENEATH THE BELL

THE CAT FOUND THE BELL BY SCENT, NOT SIGHT.

It had wandered behind the altar, past the folded cushions and old robes that hadn't been touched in seasons, into a place where the air smelled of dust and something older—something that felt like it had been waiting to be noticed.

The bell sat in a wooden crate, half-covered by a worn cloth.

Small and dull, without ornament or shine, the kind of bell that wasn't meant to call anyone, but to mark the moment after something had already shifted.

The cat circled it once, slowly, drawn not by sound, but by the weight of the silence that surrounded it.

Leaning closer, it pressed its nose to the cool surface, tracing the edge until its whiskers brushed the underside —and there it stopped.

Faint lines, almost invisible in the dim light, a single name etched just deep enough to be real, just shallow enough to be missed by anyone not looking for it.

The cat wasn't sure it had been.

It read the shape again, letting its breath slow as if the name carried a weight beyond language.

It pressed one paw to the base of the bell, just gently enough to feel the cool metal shift beneath its weight.

The bell did not ring.

Behind the cat, a monk appeared in the doorway.

He stood there, watching.

When he finally spoke, his voice was soft, almost uncertain.

"I found that name once, too," he said, not as if he were offering an answer, but as if he were confessing something to the empty room.

The cat flicked its tail but stayed facing the bell.

The monk leaned against the frame, his gaze drifting toward the fading light.

"I never spoke it aloud," he whispered after a while.

"Not because I didn't know it...but because I wasn't sure it was ever mine to speak."

The cat stayed there a moment longer, feeling the air grow heavier with something unsaid.

And then, without striking the bell, without looking back, it stood and walked away.

The bell did not ring that night.

Nor the next.

But the air around it seemed to hum just a little differently—as if the name had been carried back into silence, leaving only the question of who had left it there in the first place.

11

THE MIRROR CRACKED IN MOONLIGHT

THE CAT RETURNED TO THE ROOM IT HADN'T visited in a long time.

It wasn't clear why—just that something pulled it there, the way a leaf follows wind without knowing where it started.

The paper screens trembled softly as the night breeze moved through them, the scent of damp cedar rising from the floorboards. The air itself seemed to remember something.

The mirror was still there.

Round. Simple. Clean, though no one cleaned it.

But now, a crack ran through it.

Thin. Barely visible. Like a hairline on still water.

The cat approached slowly, each step deliberate as if the

floor might give way beneath its paws. The stillness in the room deepened, like the hush before a bell is struck.

It looked into the glass.

Its reflection stared back. But something was wrong—almost immediately.

The reflected cat blinked out of rhythm.

A paw lifted when the real cat stood perfectly still.

The cat tilted its head, ears twitching.

The mirror-cat moved—but not in answer.

It crouched, its tail flicking once, twice. Then it leapt —vanishing.

There, beneath a plum tree heavy with late-spring blossoms, a tiny bird trembled on a branch.

A breeze stirred the petals. One fell. Then another.

The cat blinked. The room around it held only silence and moonlight. No tree. No bird.

And yet... it knew that tree.

Or thought it did.

A feather floated across the mirror's surface, dissolving as it touched the widening crack.

A soft, brittle sound—like the crack deepening ever so slightly.

The cat pressed a paw to the glass.

The image shifted.

Now the mirror held the vision of a dimly lit hall. A monk sat on a cushion, his back to the cat. His body shook—not from laughter, but from something quieter, heavier. His shoulders trembled with each silent sob.

The mirror-cat curled itself at the monk's side, its presence soft as breath.

The cat outside the glass felt a strange tightness in its chest. It did not remember this moment.

Or maybe it did.

But not like this. Not in this shape. Not in this silence.

A whisper of unease threaded through its fur. Its tail flicked once, uncertainly.

And then...

Another shift.

Now it saw itself—smaller, soaked, shivering.

A tiny kitten beneath a broken eave, rain slashing down in sheets.

Wind howled through empty alleys, cold and sharp. The kitten's fur clung to its thin body, too small to withstand the storm.

A soft whimper escaped the real cat's throat—barely a sound at all, as if remembering something long buried beneath a thousand ordinary days.

It backed away, claws scraping lightly against the wooden floor. But it didn't leave.

Not yet.

A soft footstep. Bare.

The cat turned its head toward the doorway.

There stood a monk—old, bent slightly to one side as if the years had collected more on one shoulder than the other. He carried nothing but a small bundle of cloth in one hand. His face, half in shadow, bore no expression.

Without fully stepping into the room, the monk spoke,

"Do you know how the mirror came to be here?"

The cat did not move.

The monk tilted his head toward the glass.

"They say it was made from the surface of a frozen lake. A single winter night, long ago. The craftsman used the breath of the dying moon to shape it... and sealed inside whatever the lake reflected last."

The cat's ears twitched.

The monk smiled faintly, as if at some private joke, then left.

Soft footsteps faded into the hallway, leaving nothing but the hum of silence behind.

The cat looked back toward the mirror.

Its reflection was gone.

Only the crack remained—running clean through an empty surface that now caught the moonlight in its fracture. A thin line of silver widening so slowly it seemed the glass itself might sigh.

The cat stood for a moment longer.

Then it turned.

And walked away.

12

THE DOG WHO REMEMBERED

THE CAT WAS STRETCHED OUT IN A PATCH OF afternoon sun near the old gate when it heard the sound —a slow, uneven rhythm in the dust.

The cat opened one eye.

The dog stood at the edge of the path, one back paw dragging slightly with each step, leaving a faint, broken line in the earth behind it.

Its fur was patchy in places, ears slightly bent, but its eyes —its eyes were steady, bright in a way the cat almost recognized but didn't dare name.

The dog lowered itself with a soft grunt.

"I wondered if you'd still come here," the dog said quietly.

The cat flicked its tail, but didn't reply.

The dog shifted its weight, exhaling a little harder than before.

"We used to watch the temple walls, you and I," it continued, the words coming slowly, as if testing their own shape.

"You on the east side...me on the west. Every morning, by the bell."

The words stirred something deeper this time—not a thought, but a flicker of sensation.

And then, like a sudden jolt, the cat remembered.

The east wall, bathed in morning light, its shadow just beginning to pull across the courtyard.

The dog—younger then, eager in ways the cat never quite understood—had stood tall by the west gate, head high, chest forward, as if holding back an invisible army only it could see.

The cat, silent as breath, had watched from the far side,

One morning, a single leaf had blown between them, spinning lazily in the breeze.

Not prey. Not threat.

Just a leaf, dancing the line between their posts.

The dog had shifted first, paws light on the stone.

The cat had watched without moving, waiting for the leaf to drift closer.

And when it did, neither of them chased it.

They had simply stood there, facing each other across the courtyard, watching the leaf settle in the center of the space between them.

The memory passed.

The dog let out a dry, half-laugh.

"Maybe you don't remember," it whispered.

"Or maybe you do...and you're just better at leaving things behind."

A small leaf scraped across the stones between them, curling toward the edge of the gate.

This time, the dog didn't follow it.

Its gaze stayed steady, as if it knew better than to chase what was already gone.

"I had a dream," the dog murmured after a long pause.

"You were on the roof, watching the stars."

The cat shifted its weight—feeling the ground beneath its paws.

The dog smiled softly, seeing the small movement.

"You always did that...when you didn't want to answer."

The space between them held.

Finally, the dog stood, its limp more pronounced in the silence.

"Or maybe," it whispered, "I've been chasing the wrong memory."

Without waiting for a reply, it turned toward the trees, dragging its broken line behind it.

The cat watched until the sound disappeared, ears tilted forward, body unmoving.

And when the dust had fully settled, the cat stood.

It walked the long curve of the temple walls until it reached the east gate.

There, in the place where the light used to fall, it lowered itself to the ground.

Just sitting, facing the empty courtyard, as if listening to something no one else could hear.

And somewhere deep in the night, beneath breath and bone, the bell began to ring.

13

THE TEACUP THAT SPILLED TIME

It happened during a quiet afternoon in the temple kitchen.

Nothing unusual. Just a novice boiling water, humming softly to himself. A single teacup resting on the edge of the counter. The cat watched from the top of a nearby shelf, half-asleep, paws tucked beneath its chest.

The novice turned away for a moment to check the pot.

That was when the teacup began to fall.

The cat saw it tilt. Just a little. Just enough.

But instead of dropping quickly to the floor, it seemed to hang there—caught mid-air. Not floating, exactly. Not frozen. Just... pausing. As if something had gently pressed pause on the world.

The cup leaned further. Tea hovered near the rim, but didn't spill.

The cat jumped down and padded closer.

It wasn't in a hurry. It sat beside the cup and looked. The air around it felt different—thicker, quieter. Like the space between two thoughts that haven't quite decided what to become.

The cat circled once. Tilted its head.

The cup stayed exactly where it was.

Time passed—though it didn't feel as if it had.

The water in the pot behind the novice began to boil. The bubbles popped softly. Steam filled the air. The cat stayed where it was, unmoving.

Then, just as the novice turned around, the cup completed its fall.

It hit the stone floor and cracked. Not violently. Not with drama. Just a clean, soft sound. The tea spread out in a thin puddle.

The novice blinked.

He looked at the floor. Then at the shelf where the cat had been.

The cat had already wandered off, leaving only a single pawprint in the wet stone near the broken pieces.

That evening, the cat found a shard of the cup by the doorway. It sniffed it, turned it over with its paw once, then left it there.

No interest in putting it back together.

14

THE MONK WHO DREAMED OF FUR

It was the youngest monk who struggled the most.

Though his robes were clean and his posture straight, his mind fidgeted like a sparrow in a basket. For weeks, he had sat in the zendo as still as he could manage, yet inside —churning. Counting breaths, losing count. Watching thoughts, only to find himself tangled in them.

He had started reading too much. Memorizing sayings. Rehearsing questions he might ask the abbot. He found himself trapped in the net of understanding, tightening the knot with every effort to untangle it.

One evening, after failing to find stillness once again, he wandered the temple grounds under the pale moon.

The cat watched him from a low stone wall, tail flicking lazily.

The monk sighed, bowed toward it half-playfully, and returned to his room, folding himself into restless sleep.

And then—

He was no longer the boy in the robe, but something smaller, lower to the earth. He felt the sun-warmed stone beneath four delicate paws. Each step rippled up his limbs like quiet thunder.

The wind carried stories—sour plum blossoms, old sandalwood, the musky breath of earth.

He could feel the air through the long whiskers that now extended from his face. The flick of an ear felt like poetry. He moved without deciding to move. Every motion was answerless and complete.

The temple wall stretched before him, a vast highway of ancient stone. He leapt, weightless. Not a thought arose —not even the thought of not thinking. He was wind. He was muscle. He was stone and paw.

And when he paused on the rooftop, tail flicking under a star-pricked sky, he turned back and saw himself—the boy in robes—blinking up at him with startled eyes. But somehow, those were his eyes too. Both looking, both being looked at.

The world folded into itself. He could not tell who was dreaming whom.

He awoke before dawn, the taste of stone still on his tongue.

When he rose to walk, the ground met him differently. He felt the smooth coldness of the floor through the thin fabric of his sandals, the dampness of dew clinging to his skin as he stepped outside.

In the courtyard, the cat lay sprawled in a patch of early sunlight, as if waiting.

He approached slowly and knelt. For a moment, he did nothing—no reaching, no calling, no words.

The cat opened one eye. Their gazes met—not as monk and animal, not as question and answer, but as two shapes in the same unfolding dream.

Neither moved. Neither needed to.

When the bell sounded for morning chores, the cat stretched long and languid, leapt from the stones, and disappeared around the corner.

Later that night, while the others slept, the monk climbed quietly onto the temple roof.

Sitting cross-legged where tile met sky, he breathed the night air without trying to measure it. The stars above shimmered without needing names.

And though no one could see him, his tail—if he'd had one—might have flicked just once in the dark.

He sat without seeking, without striving.

He simply sat.

And the temple, the cat, the boy, and the sky all breathed as one.

15

THE FISH WITHOUT A SHADOW

THE CAT HAD SEEN FISH BEFORE—SMALL ONES, quick and nervous, flashing like silver leaves beneath the surface.

But this one was different.

It moved slowly, almost lazily, gliding through the clear water near the edge of the dock.

And it had no shadow.

The cat narrowed its eyes and leaned forward, peering closer.

No outline beneath it. No dark shape on the stones below.

Just the fish—bright, perfect, and floating alone in the light.

It watched the fish circle again and again, each pass

slower than the last, as if the fish were aware of being watched.

As if it had come to be seen.

A monk stood a few steps away, holding a bamboo rod loosely in one hand. The line hung slack over the water, the hook just beneath the surface, unmoving.

The cat flicked its tail and crept forward, low to the dock, every muscle alive with something it couldn't quite name —curiosity, hunger, or something thinner, like the edge of a dream starting to fray.

The fish drifted closer to the hook.

The monk's fingers tensed ever so slightly on the rod.

The cat held its breath.

Then, without warning, the fish turned and struck.

The rod bent sharply.

The line stretched tight.

For one long moment, everything held in place— balanced between tension and release.

And then the line snapped, softly, as if it had given up.

The fish vanished into the dark water.

The dock rocked gently beneath the sudden emptiness.

The monk lowered the rod, not with frustration, but with something quieter—a kind of surrender, like someone who had known the outcome all along.

He turned and walked back toward the temple without a word.

The cat didn't follow.

It stayed at the edge of the dock, staring into the water— not searching for the fish, not waiting for its return, just sitting there, listening to the strange stillness it left behind.

16

THE DOOR WITH NO INSIDE

THE DOOR HAD ALWAYS BEEN THERE.

Tucked in the far corner of the meditation hall—faded wood, no handle, no lock, no hinges anyone could see. Just a door-shaped outline, like someone had drawn it quickly and forgotten to finish.

The monks never mentioned it. They walked past without looking.

But the cat noticed.

One morning, it padded quietly across the hall and sat in front of it.

It stared.

The door didn't move.

The cat sniffed along the edges. No scent. It pressed its paw gently against the wood. Nothing shifted. No creak, no give. The surface was cool and still.

The cat came back the next day.

And the day after that.

It tried crawling under. Scratching. Nudging. Meowing once, then again. At one point, it leapt onto a nearby shelf and launched itself toward the top of the frame.

It bounced off and landed on the floor with a soft thud.

Still, the door remained.

Each time, the cat sat longer. Not in defeat, but in quiet attention.

By the end of the week, it wasn't scratching anymore. It was just... sitting. Breathing. Watching.

Hours passed.

Light moved across the floor.

Outside, the wind stirred the trees. A bell rang once in the distance.

Then, without reason, the cat stood and walked away.

It didn't look back.

That night, it slept in the garden under the open sky. The air was cool. The grass bent gently beneath its weight.

Before its eyes closed, a thought—not quite a thought—passed through.

Maybe there had never been a door.

Or maybe the cat had never been outside it to begin with.

17

THE THREAD IN THE CAT'S MOUTH

THE CAT DIDN'T KNOW WHEN IT HAD STARTED.

The thread was already in its mouth when it woke—thin and pale, light as breath, stretching out behind it into the dark.

At first, the cat walked without thinking, weaving quietly through doorways and across stone paths, the thread trailing behind like something half-alive.

It moved easily at first, sliding across the floor with hardly any weight at all.

But as the cat wandered deeper into the temple, something shifted.

The thread began to resist—

not sharply, not enough to pull it back—

but with just enough tension to make the cat pause.

It bit down gently, testing the pull.

The thread held firm.

The cat stood still, ears flicking, feeling the quiet hum of something pulling from the other end.

It took another step.

And another.

With each movement, the thread pulled a little more, not enough to stop it, but enough to remind it that something unseen was waiting.

The cat reached the doorway of the meditation hall and stopped there, its body leaning slightly forward, its breath growing shallow.

It knew, somehow, without needing to understand—if it held on, the pull might never stop.

But if it let go, the thread would vanish.

The cat stood frozen in that small hesitation. It stood on the edge of holding or letting go—until, with a breath it hadn't known it was holding, it let go.

The thread slipped from its mouth, so light it seemed to dissolve before it even touched the ground.

The cat watched the empty air where the thread had been, its tongue pressing against the roof of its mouth as if searching for the shape of something already gone.

It stayed there, unmoving.

And when it finally did, the temple felt lighter.

Reflection Questions

FOR BEGINNERS

What if the way forward feels like forgetting where
you've been?

What have you learned through absence that you
couldn't learn through presence?

What happens when something reveals more of itself
than you were ready for?

How do you live with what feels unfinished, unresolved,
or unnamed?

PART III
The Cat Who Disappeared

EVERYTHING CHANGES. EVERYTHING IS
SACRED. EVERYTHING DISAPPEARS.

Shunryu Suzuki

18

THE BOWL WITH NO REFLECTION

It wasn't anyone's bowl.

Or maybe it had been. Long ago.

But now it sat at the edge of the garden, half-buried in fallen leaves, glazed a soft green and chipped at the rim. Someone might have left it there after tea. Or forgotten it during chores. No one claimed it.

Except the rain.

The bowl filled slowly, drop by drop, day by day. Some mornings the water was clear, perfectly still. Other days it held bits of leaf, a petal, the sky.

The cat found it by accident.

It sniffed the rim, then sat beside it—not to drink, but to look.

The bowl didn't shimmer. It didn't reflect anything important. It just held what it was given.

The next day, the cat returned.

Then again.

And again.

It became a quiet routine.

One morning, while the cat was sitting beside the bowl, an old monk passed by on his way to the compost pile.

He slowed. Looked down at the cat. Then at the bowl.

He blinked.

Then reached into his robe, pulled out a single radish, and tossed it over his shoulder into the bushes.

"Didn't see anything," he muttered, and kept walking.

The cat didn't move.

Neither did the bowl.

Over time, the glaze wore thin. The cracks deepened. Water leaked, slowly at first, then faster. Some days the bowl was full. Other days it was nearly empty. Once, a bird tried to bathe in it and tipped it halfway over.

The cat watched all of this without judgment.

It never drank from the bowl.

Never tried to stop the changes.

Only returned.

One morning, after a long night of rain, the cat arrived to

find the bowl overturned. A puddle had formed beside it, but the bowl itself was empty.

No leaves. No sky.

Just earth.

The cat sat beside it for a long time, then turned away and walked into the trees.

The next morning, the bowl was gone.

Not moved. Not broken.

Gone.

Only a soft ring in the grass remained, where the ground had learned the shape of something that once held the rain.

19

THE WHISPER IN THE HALLWAY

IT BEGAN WITH THE SMALLEST SOUND—SO faint it could have been imagined.

Not breath. Not words.

Something thinner, like fabric shifting in an empty room, or the pause between footsteps.

The novice sat up on his futon, heart beating a little too loud in the quiet.

He held his breath, listening.

There it was again—closer this time, just beyond the paper-thin wall.

He slid the door open slowly, bare feet sinking into the cool wood of the hallway.

The air smelled faintly of old cedar and night rain.

Moonlight pressed softly through the shoji, turning the floor pale and uneven.

He stood there for a long moment, half certain he should turn back.

But the whisper stirred again.

He stepped forward, past the bell rope swaying slightly in the draft, past the cracked plaster he had promised to mend.

Each step felt slower than the last, as if the hallway had grown longer while he wasn't looking.

And then he saw it.

At the far end, beneath the window where the moon hung low, the cat sat watching him.

Still. Silent.

Its eyes caught the light in a way that made him shiver.

It didn't move.

The novice tried to speak, but no sound left his tongue.

The whisper rose again, not in his ears this time—but *inside* him.

He felt his body tense, one foot frozen between going back and stepping closer.

For a moment, the whole hallway seemed to tilt.

He closed his eyes, just for a heartbeat, to steady himself.

When he opened them, the cat was gone.

No pawsteps. No sound.

He stood there, unsure how long.

When he finally turned back toward his room, he felt something trailing behind him.

20

THE CUSHION THAT VANISHED

It wasn't the softest cushion in the temple.

It wasn't the newest, or the cleanest.

But it sat just right.

Low to the ground, edges worn soft by years of folding bodies, sunlight brushing it each morning through the south window.

The monks never claimed it as theirs, but everyone knew its weight.

A longer bow.

A quiet glance.

A breath held just a moment longer when someone arrived early enough to sit there.

The cat knew it, too.

Some mornings, it would curl itself into that small, sunlit space before anyone else arrived—tail wrapped tight, breath slow and steady, filling the room with something the monks never dared disturb.

They sat around it, making do on folded robes, hard floors, empty space.

No one spoke of ownership.

The cushion belonged to no one.

But it anchored them all.

Until one morning, it was gone.

The cat was late that day.

It stopped in the doorway, ears tilting toward the quiet.

The monks held their breath without meaning to.

The cat walked slowly to the empty patch of floor, stood for a long moment, then sat down.

The monks gathered quietly, each one settling around the empty space, careful not to disturb the silence hanging between them.

No one joked.

No one filled the air with easy words.

It felt as if the whole room had shifted—tilted just slightly toward something they couldn't name.

The next day, someone brought a new cushion.

Placed it in the same spot.

Same shape. Almost the same color.

It looked right.

But something in the air pulled back.

No one sat on it.

Not that day. Not the next.

The cat returned as before, moving to the edge of the space, never touching the new cushion, never filling the absence.

It sat beside it, as if guarding something too light to hold.

Eventually, the new cushion was moved to another room.

The empty space remained.

So did the cat.

21

THE CAT'S LAST PAWPRINT

THE RAIN HAD FALLEN ALL NIGHT.

By morning, the stones of the courtyard were slick and shining. Leaves stuck to the ground. The air was cool and still.

A monk crossing the path stopped suddenly.

There, in the middle of the stone walkway, was a single pawprint.

Clear. Small. Recent.

Just one.

No trail behind it. No second step. And no cat.

He bent down. The print wasn't dry. But there was no mud. Just the soft indent of a paw, pressed into wet stone like a pressed flower.

Another monk walked up beside him.

"That wasn't there earlier," he said.

"It's fresh," said the first.

They looked around. No cat. No footprints anywhere else.

"Could've been from yesterday," someone offered.

"Then why's it still wet?" the other replied.

Later, someone found a second pawprint—this one on the wooden porch of the meditation hall. It hadn't rained there.

A third print appeared in the hallway outside the bell tower.

One monk washed it away.

The next morning, it was back.

The cat hadn't been seen in days.

Eventually, the prints stopped appearing.

But by then, no one really believed they were ever just prints.

Someone began leaving a bowl of water by the first one. Another monk left a folded scrap of cloth, as if for drying paws that never touched the floor.

No one spoke of it too loudly. But they all walked a little more carefully.

And when the final pawprint faded—so faint it was hard

to know if it had ever been there at all—they still stepped around the spot.

22

THE CAT WHO WAS PAINTED INTO THE WALL

THEY UNCOVERED THE MURAL BY ACCIDENT, during repairs in the east corridor, when a novice wiped a damp cloth across what had always been just another soot-stained wall.

Underneath the dust, lines began to appear—soft, worn brushstrokes, a seated monk beneath a tree, hands resting in his lap, eyes half-closed, as if listening to something just out of reach.

An elder paused behind the novice and nodded slowly.

"Ah," he murmured, "The Sitting One."

He didn't explain.

He walked on, leaving the novice standing there, alone with the wall.

It wasn't until later—when the light shifted across the floor—that the novice noticed something more.

Low in the mural, tucked among the roots of the tree, a cat.

Small. Curled tight.

No more than a few brushstrokes, as if the painter had almost hidden it there on purpose.

The novice leaned in, heart quickening.

"Was that always there?" he asked aloud.

The elder glanced back, squinted, and shook his head.

"I don't see anything," he said, then turned away again.

But the novice did see it.

He returned the next day. And the day after.

Each time, the cat had shifted.

Sometimes it faced left. Sometimes right.

Once, it appeared to be standing, its back arched, eyes fixed on something beyond the edge of the painting.

The novice began to wake early, slipping into the corridor before the others stirred, just to see what the cat had become.

He stopped asking questions.

The more he watched, the more the cat seemed to move —not just in posture, but in presence.

It felt alive.

And then, one morning, it was gone.

The entire mural.

The wall was bare, smooth and pale, as if no hand had ever touched it.

The novice reached out, fingertips grazing the empty surface, as if the texture might give something back.

But there was nothing.

Only stillness.

Only air.

He stood there far longer than he meant to, waiting for something to shift again.

But nothing came.

At last, he lowered himself to the floor, right where the cat had once been.

And though the others passed by without stopping, some glanced toward the empty wall, their breath catching as if they, too, almost remembered something.

In time, a few began sitting beside him, not asking, not naming, not searching.

Just sitting.

And no one—not once—said the wall had never held a thing.

23

THE CAT WHO ANSWERED NOTHING

THE MONK HAD CARRIED THE QUESTION FOR years.

Not in a scroll, not in a notebook—but in his mind.

It had first come to him during his first year at the temple, though he couldn't say exactly when. Back then, it had felt important—something large and complex, threaded with philosophy and meaning. It had taken the shape of a grand theological inquiry about the nature of emptiness, life, death, and what lay beyond words.

He had written it down once, covering an entire page with careful strokes. But the next morning, when he read it again, it felt hollow. He burned the page before morning zazen.

Years passed. The question softened. Grew simpler. He stopped trying to phrase it. It became more of a weight than a thought—something he carried not with his mind anymore, but in his body, worn smooth like a stone in his robe pocket.

Still, it troubled him.

During one winter sesshin, the master assigned him a koan: *"Show me your original face, before your parents were born."*

The monk wanted to bring the question forward then— to offer it as his answer. But each time he opened his mouth, nothing came. Only hesitation.

After the interview, he stayed behind, bowing so low his forehead touched the wooden floor. He pressed his palms together, feeling the question ache like a knot in his chest.

One night, unable to sleep, he wandered to the old cedar bridge beyond the temple wall. He leaned on the railing and watched the dark water slide below. After a moment, he whispered the question aloud.

The sound of it seemed smaller than he remembered.

So small, it almost didn't seem worth asking anymore.

Then, one evening, just as the sun slid low behind the western ridge, he saw the cat.

It was sitting beneath the old stone lantern in the garden, half in shadow, half in light. Its fur caught the fading glow, every whisker outlined like a brushstroke on parchment. Its tail flicked once, then settled. The breeze moved gently through the temple trees, and the monk noticed, oddly, that the cat's breath seemed to rise and fall with the wind itself—as if there was no difference between the two.

Without thinking, he stood and stepped outside.

Each step felt as if it had already been taken long ago.

He approached slowly, stopping a few paces away.

He bowed, deeper than he ever had before.

When he raised his head, the cat was watching him.

Calm. Unmoving. Clear as water.

And so he asked once more.

Not to seek approval. Not to find resolution.

But to let the question go, fully, completely.

The cat blinked once.

Then stood, stretched, turned, and walked away.

The monk remained standing for a long while, not knowing whether something had been received—or quietly taken.

That night, he returned to the same spot and sat cross-legged on the stone path.

He didn't try to remember the question.

He didn't try to forget it either.

He let it drift—like a leaf on water, neither grasped nor released.

The moon rose, then fell.

Dawn began to color the sky.

The birds began their soft calls in the trees.

And as the first light touched his shoulders, the monk felt something loosen in his body.

He took a deep breath.

And smiled.

24

THE CAT WHO SAT BEHIND THE MOON

THE DREAMS BEGAN IN EARLY AUTUMN.

A young monk started waking with the same image in his mind each morning: the full moon, round and unmoving, hanging low over the temple roof. And behind it— just barely visible—was the cat.

Not on the moon. Not beside it.

Behind it.

Hidden by light. Half there. More suggestion than shape.

In the first dream, the monk tried to speak. No words came. Only the stillness of night, and the feeling that something was waiting just beyond what could be seen.

He mentioned the dream to an older monk the next morning.

"What do you think it means?" he asked.

The elder shrugged. "Don't turn it into something it isn't."

That night, the dream returned.

But this time, the cat's eyes were open—two glimmers, impossibly bright, burning like stars behind the pale moon's glow. The monk awoke with the image seared behind his eyelids.

The next night, the cat blinked. Slowly. Once.

By the third night, there was sound. Faint, almost imagined—a low, steady purr. When he awoke, the sound stayed in his chest, vibrating softly beneath his ribs.

As the week unfolded, the moon in his dream began to shift—waxing, waning, splitting into crescents and vanishing to dark. Yet the cat remained, always in its place, never moving, never more than a whisper of form behind the light.

The young monk became restless.

During the day, he wandered the temple grounds in secret.

He sat beneath the bell tower, peering upward for hours.

He traced the moon's reflection in puddles and tea bowls with trembling fingers.

He even began to sketch crude outlines of the cat in the margins of his sutra scrolls, hiding them quickly when footsteps approached.

His tasks slipped through his hands like smoke. He left the incense unlit. He missed the morning chants. He nodded off during scripture readings. The older monks began to notice, though none said a word.

And yet, each evening when he settled into zazen, his breath would steady. His thoughts would settle. The search would fall away like dust from his robes.

For those few moments, he was simply sitting—present and empty.

But still the dreams returned.

One evening, as the leaves began to fall, the monk sat alone beneath the silver glow of the autumn moon.

And when the cat appeared behind it, as it had so many nights before, the monk did something he had not yet dared.

He spoke to it.

Softly.

Almost without sound.

"Why do you hide behind the moon?" he asked.

In the dream, the cat blinked.

Once. Nothing more.

The monk felt his breath catch. He waited for something —anything—yet nothing came.

No words. No movement.

Only that single, deliberate blink.

From that night on, the monk stopped searching.

He no longer climbed the bell tower.

He no longer scratched secret drawings in the scrolls.

He no longer chased reflections in puddles or bowls.

Instead, he began to sit. Night after night. Alone in the courtyard. Facing the sky.

Until, one night, the moon did not rise.

The clouds hung heavy and black.

He sat anyway.

Long after the others had gone inside.

Long after the night had thickened into silence.

And there—beneath the weight of an empty sky—he felt something.

A presence.

Not behind the moon.

Everywhere.

Everything.

He lowered his head and smiled—not because he understood, but because there was nothing left to understand.

That night, he didn't dream.

And the sky—dark and bare—felt full.

25

THE MONK WHO STOPPED ASKING

HE HAD ALWAYS ASKED QUESTIONS.

About the nature of thought. About non-attachment. About the difference between stillness and waiting.

He was respected for his mind. And quietly avoided during meals.

When the others sat in zazen, he scribbled in a small notebook. When they walked in silence, he muttered things like, "But what does silence respond to?"

He wasn't disliked.

But just his presence alone was exhausting.

Then one morning, he said nothing.

He ate in silence. Walked without commentary. During sitting, he sat.

The first day, the others assumed he was sick.

The second day, curious.

By the third, someone asked him gently, "Are you alright?"

He nodded.

And smiled.

The notebook remained closed.

Later that week, a novice swore he saw the cat enter the monk's room.

No one else saw it.

But no one doubted it.

After that, the monk grew even quieter.

He bowed more deeply. He swept the walkway twice. Once, he stood outside in the rain and said nothing for so long that the Abbot closed the window rather than interrupt.

Then, one morning, he was gone.

Not missing—just gone.

His robe was folded neatly on his mat. The notebook, blank.

No farewell. No trace.

Someone left a bowl of rice on the step.

Another placed a stone beside it.

Nothing was said aloud.

But for weeks afterward, the others found themselves speaking less, and bowing more.

Reflection Questions

What has disappeared from your life but still seems to leave a presence behind?

What in your life have you passed by many times without truly seeing?

What if what you long for is already here, just out of reach?

What questions are you carrying that cannot be answered with words?

PART IV
Moonlight Without Shape

TO STUDY THE SELF IS TO FORGET THE
SELF. TO FORGET THE SELF IS TO BE
AWAKENED BY ALL THINGS.

Eihei Dōgen

26

THE CAT IN THE TEACUP

THE FIRST TIME THE MONK SAW IT, HE TOLD himself it was nothing—just steam, just light, a trick of the eye after a long night without sleep.

But the next day, it appeared again.

The cat, small and still, perfectly reflected in the dark surface of his tea.

Not beside the cup.

Not near the tray.

Inside the tea itself, as if it had been waiting there all along.

He looked up quickly, half-expecting to find it sitting just beyond his reach.

But there was nothing.

Only the quiet hum of morning, the air soft and ordinary, the cup growing cooler in his hands.

He glanced back down.

The reflection hadn't moved.

For days he tried to ignore it.

He turned the cup away from him, drank quickly, kept his eyes on the floor.

But the reflection always returned—calm, patient, unchanging.

And with each passing day, something inside him grew heavier.

It wasn't fear exactly, but something thinner—like standing at the edge of a question he couldn't bring himself to ask.

He began pouring more slowly, watching the steam rise and clear, waiting for the moment the cat would appear again.

It never startled him.

But it never felt quite real, either.

One morning, after weeks of circling the same hesitation, he did not turn the cup away.

He stared straight into the reflection, his hands trembling just enough to ripple the surface.

Without breaking his gaze, he lifted the cup to his lips and drank.

The reflection scattered into waves of light, gone before the taste reached his tongue.

The next day, he poured again, half-expecting to see it return.

But there was nothing.

Just tea.

Plain and still.

He sat with the empty cup in his hands for a long time, longer than he could explain.

And for the first time, the emptiness felt enough.

27

THE ECHO BENEATH THE FLOORBOARDS

THE FIRST TIME THEY HEARD IT, THE MONKS thought it was the wind.

A low, steady hum rising up from beneath the floorboards of the old meditation hall—so soft it was hard to tell if it was real, or just imagined.

No one mentioned it at first.

But over the next few days, it returned. Always at dusk. Always beneath the floor.

Not loud enough to disturb. Just enough to make the air feel heavier, like someone was sitting under the floor, breathing very slowly.

One of the novices, a quiet boy who had arrived only weeks before, seemed unable to ignore it. While the others filed out after evening meditation, he stayed behind, pressing his ear to the wooden floor.

At first, they teased him gently.

"Hear anything interesting down there?" someone asked.

The novice only nodded, but said nothing.

By the end of the week, he began bringing his mat to the back corner of the hall, as close to the sound as he could. He lay on his side, ear against the floor, breathing with the rhythm of whatever was humming below.

One night, a senior monk approached and sat beside him.

"What do you hear?" he asked softly.

The novice waited a long time before answering.

"Not sound," he whispered. "Not exactly."

The older monk frowned, but didn't press.

In the mornings, the sound was gone.

In the afternoons, nothing.

Only at dusk, when the light turned thin and the air seemed to hold its breath, would it return.

Then one evening, the sound didn't come.

The novice lay there anyway, ear pressed to wood, body motionless.

It didn't return the next day either.

Or the day after that.

But the novice kept returning, long after the others had stopped noticing.

And though the hall fell silent, he stayed listening.

28

THE QUESTION THAT NEVER ARRIVED

It began, as these things often do, with a commotion in the courtyard.

The messenger—a bumbling villager, known more for his mispronounced proverbs than his wisdom—burst through the temple gates, clutching a crumpled scroll above his head like a treasure rescued from fire.

"It *flew* into my hands!" he declared breathlessly, wobbling as he tried to catch his breath. "Like a drunk butterfly on its last sip of sake!"

The monks, drawn by the noise, gathered with cautious curiosity. The abbot approached, folding his hands with the patient gravity of one who has already lived through too many of the villager's antics.

But this time, something was different.

There—on the outer wrapping of the scroll—were three

small characters, brushed in soft black ink: the name of their temple.

The villager lowered his voice, leaning in as if revealing a state secret.

"I was told this scroll carries a question," he whispered, eyes wide, "meant for the cat."

A hushed breath swept through the monks like a breeze through dry leaves.

Without waiting for permission, he dramatically unrolled the scroll, holding it high for all to see.

Blank.

Not a single mark. No words. No symbols. Just the soft weave of handmade fibers, pale and empty.

The silence cracked as one monk, eager to demonstrate his insight, squinted until his face contorted into something between enlightenment and indigestion.

"I see it," he muttered.

Another sniffed the scroll noisily, declaring, "Invisible ink! The answer reveals itself only to those with the purest nostrils!"

A third, seated cross-legged with exaggerated serenity, announced, "It is a test... of our Emptiness Quotient. We must meditate until the meaning reveals itself—or until we no longer care."

The abbot sighed.

And that's when the cat, unnoticed until now, padded silently into the hall. Without so much as a glance at the gathering, it leapt gracefully onto the altar. One soft paw reached out, tapped the scroll, and with a flick, sent it skittering across the polished wood floor.

Gasps rippled through the hall. Some monks nodded solemnly, as if this act contained the heart of all teachings. Others bowed their heads, murmuring, "The cat has answered."

The abbot, watching the absurdity unfold, let out something that hadn't passed his lips in years—a chuckle.

He picked up the scroll, held it over the brazier, and with a glint of mischief in his eye, let the paper catch flame.

"The question," he declared, "was too shy to stay."

The monks watched the ashes curl upward, rising into the darkened rafters like tiny grey butterflies returning to the wind. The cat, seemingly satisfied, circled twice and settled atop the warm altar, curling into sleep as though nothing more needed to be said.

And though the scroll had turned to smoke, and the hall slowly emptied, the weight of the moment hung in the air—vibrant, ridiculous, and somehow complete.

Outside, the wind stirred again.

The monks bowed.

And the cat dreamed on.

29

THE MONK WHO CALLED THE CAT BACKWARDS

No one knew when he had started.

One evening, as the last light fell across the stones, the quiet monk—the one who never spoke unless spoken to—was heard whispering something under his breath as he walked the temple paths alone.

It took days before anyone noticed he was repeating the cat's name—not forward, but backwards.

Not loud. Not playful.

Just a low murmur, soft enough to almost disappear into the wind.

At first, they let it pass without comment.

Monks had their rituals.

Who could say what stirred in a man after so much silence?

But the chanting didn't stop.

Night after night, he circled the temple grounds, his feet tracing the same worn paths, the name spilling quietly from his lips, reversed into something that sounded less like a word, and more like a sound being pulled back into the dark.

And then...the remembering began.

One monk claimed he had seen the cat in the garden at dawn—sitting exactly where it used to sit, tail curled neatly around its feet.

Another insisted he had heard the faintest scratch at the door during the night—a sound he would have sworn was real, except the door had not been touched in months.

Soon, more memories surfaced.

Moments they couldn't place in time.

Conversations they were sure had already happened, or maybe hadn't yet.

The air grew heavy with the strange hum of almost remembering.

Or almost forgetting.

Still, the chanting monk never explained.

He never looked up when they passed him on the path.

He never changed his pace.

He never missed a step.

It was as if he were walking in a circle no one else could see.

Some began to wonder—was he calling the cat back?

Or was he walking with something none of them could follow?

And then, one morning, the chanting stopped.

The monk's place in the evening path remained empty.

No one asked where he had gone.

But in the nights that followed, the air felt thinner somehow—the half-formed memories slipping further away, like smoke that had never really gathered.

The monks stopped speaking of it.

And no one—not even the wind—could seem to remember how it had begun.

30

THE CAT MADE OF SMOKE

For years, no one had questioned the way the incense moved.

It rose, curled through the rafters, and disappeared.

Until one evening, when someone noticed it wasn't drifting the way it usually did.

The smoke seemed to gather—low to the floor, thicker than normal, as if caught by a draft that didn't exist. It held there, swirling slowly, pooling into something more than vapor.

One of the younger monks leaned forward, squinting.

"Do you see that?"

Someone else nodded. "It looks like..."

But the words trailed off before they landed.

The shape began to lift—long and low, like a shadow taking form.

Ears.

A tail.

The unmistakable outline of a cat.

No one moved.

The smoke drifted between the rows of seated monks, not scattering, not breaking apart. It circled once, almost like it was sniffing the air, then passed through the center of the room.

A murmur stirred in someone's throat but didn't make it to their lips.

The shape stretched—just slightly—and seemed to bow, folding into itself, thinning into nothing as the last trail of smoke dissolved.

The room stayed frozen.

No one dared to ask if the others had seen it.

No one wanted to risk being the only one.

Then, out of nowhere, the old temple dog padded into the hall, tail wagging, tongue hanging out, nails clicking softly on the floor.

Half the monks flinched, heads snapping toward the sound.

And then—soft laughter.

Not nervous. Not shaken.

Relieved.

Someone reached down to scratch behind the dog's ear.

"It's not the cat," they whispered.

And for the first time all night,

they let out their breath.

31

THE ROOM WITH NO WALLS

THE IDEA BEGAN WITH A NOVICE WHO HAD never quite found his place among the monks. His zazen posture was infamous—crooked as a leaning pine. His robes hung off his shoulder like a fisherman's net, and his yawns echoed through the halls like temple bells struck at the wrong hour.

But this novice—Jun, they called him—carried mischief like a lantern in the dark.

One morning, after toppling a water jug for the third time that week, Jun stood in the center of the garden and declared with theatrical grandeur, "Enough! I am founding *The Hall of Nothingness*—the greatest meditation hall this monastery has ever *not* seen!"

He bowed low, waved his sleeves like an actor on stage, and began dragging stones from the garden's edge. With exaggerated care, he arranged them into a lopsided, barely-square shape. The stones tilted this way and that, one noticeably smaller than the others. He stepped back, stroked his chin, and nodded as if unveiling a masterpiece.

Then, sweeping one arm toward the crooked outline, he announced, "Behold—the Boundless Hall! No roof to block the sky! No walls to trap the wind! A true hall for those brave enough to sit in... *nothing*!"

The senior monks gathered, arms crossed, eyebrows raised. One leaned toward another and whispered, "A hall needs pillars."

Another shook his head. "No, a hall needs a roof... to hold the *void* in place."

Debates ignited like dry twigs on a fire. Soon they argued over architectural absurdities—"Should the void be square or circular?" "Is an invisible roof subject to weather?" "Can the Dharma leak if there are no gutters?"

Jun, meanwhile, sat cross-legged in the middle of the crooked stones, wearing a grin so wide it seemed to stretch beyond his face. The temple cat wandered over, paused at the edge of the stone boundary, then curled up *inside* the "hall," fixing the monks with a slow, defiant blink, as if daring them to question its understanding of Zen.

Days passed. One by one, monks approached, some standing awkwardly at the edges, others stepping tentatively inside. Soon they sat together—though not without grumbling.

"This isn't proper zazen," one hissed.

Another scoffed, "Without walls, how do we know when we've entered or left?"

Yet they sat anyway.

One night, a storm blew through the garden, scattering Jun's stones into the weeds. The next morning, the monks returned, baffled. Some stood at the former edges, debating whether the hall still existed. Others paced in wide circles, mapping invisible boundaries with their fingers.

And Jun? He was already rearranging the stones—sometimes widening the space, sometimes shrinking it, sometimes stacking the stones into a tower that toppled as quickly as it rose.

Every day the hall shifted. Every day the monks bickered, sat, and adjusted themselves according to the latest "architecture."

Weeks passed like this.

Until, one morning, Jun didn't move the stones at all. In fact, there were no stones. Only the cat, sleeping where the hall had once been, tail twitching in silent amusement.

And the monks? They were sitting. Scattered. Together. Apart. No two facing the same way. No one quite "inside" or "outside." Their breath rising and falling like waves on a windless sea.

This time, they were silent.

32

THE CAT THAT DID NOT RETURN

THE CAT HAD LIVED AT THE TEMPLE FOR FIFTEEN years.

Its name had never been agreed upon.

Some called it "Whiskers". Some, "Pepsi."

Some simply called it "the cat."

It wove itself through every robe, every sandal, every quiet moment of the temple's life.

It warmed the laps of novices.

It slipped between the feet of visitors.

It curled beside the old Abbot during morning tea.

And then, one morning, it was not there.

No one saw it leave. No one found its body.

It was simply... not.

In the days that followed, the novices whispered.

"Should we search the forest?"

"Perhaps it will return."

"Maybe it has taken rebirth nearby."

The old Abbot gave no answer.

Instead, he went to the storeroom and brought out a small, worn cushion—the one the cat had claimed as its own, though it was never meant for it.

He carried it to the outer gate of the temple, the place where guests were greeted, deliveries were received, and shoes were removed.

He placed the cushion there, just beside the low wooden step, in the full light of morning.

The novices waited, but nothing happened.

No cat returned. No mystery revealed itself.

One morning, a novice approached the Abbot.

"Master, why leave the cushion by the gate? It is gone."

The Abbot nodded but said nothing.

Days passed.

Rain softened the fabric.

Wind carried bits of straw from its seams.

Still, the cushion remained.

Until, as the first breath of autumn began to stir the trees, the Abbot called the novices to the gate.

He pointed to the cushion.

"Who here can tell me what this is for?" he asked.

One novice bowed.

"To remember it."

The Abbot nodded slowly.

"And when does remembering become clinging?"

The novices fell silent.

The Abbot bent down, lifting the cushion in both hands.

He turned it over—nothing beneath it.

No fur. No scent.

Nothing at all.

"To leave this here," he said softly,

"was to let the heart ache openly.

To let the eyes see the empty space, and not turn away."

He stood.

Paused.

"But if we leave it too long, it becomes something else— not a resting place, but a refusal to move."

Without ceremony, he shook out the cushion, scattering the old straw into the wind, letting the fabric fall apart in his hands.

Then he turned toward the forest path and walked on, leaving the novices standing at the empty gate.

One by one, they bowed to the space where the cushion had been.

Not to the cushion. Not to the cat.

Not even to their grief.

But to the quiet, the ache, and the weight they could not name—light enough, perhaps, to carry.

33

THE CAT AND THE MOON

It was nearly midnight when the monk crossed the temple garden for the last time that season.

The night air felt thin, like the world was holding itself just a little farther away than usual.

He wasn't going anywhere in particular. His steps had no purpose, no rhythm. Just walking, breathing, moving.

When he reached the pond, he stopped.

The surface was still, holding the full moon like a bowl of pale light.

And just beneath the moon's reflection—the cat.

Clear as anything.

Sitting in perfect stillness, tail curled neatly around its feet, ears flicking ever so slightly in the windless night.

The monk didn't move.

Didn't blink.

He could have dropped to his knees.

Could have called out softly.

Could have leaned closer.

Instead, he took one slow breath, shifted his weight, and kept walking.

He didn't look again.

He didn't need to.

The moon remained.

The cat, perhaps, too.

Or maybe not.

Either way, the night felt full.

Reflection Questions

Can you sit with the arrival of mystery without rushing to name it?

Can you bow to something you do not understand?

What does it feel like to honor something without needing to replace it?

What if nothing needs to arrive for the moment to be complete?

Message From The Author

Thank you for taking the time to read *The Cat and The Moon*. My hope is that these stories have brought you moments of stillness, clarity, or even a small shift in perspective.

This book is part of a larger journey—to share the wisdom of Zen in a simple, accessible way so that more people can experience its teachings and find peace in their lives. In a world that often feels chaotic, even a single story can be a stepping stone to stillness.

If you found value in this book, I'd really appreciate it if you could leave an honest review. Your feedback helps others discover these teachings.

Scan the QR Code or click here to share your thoughts.

Thank you for being part of this journey.

— *Kai*

References

Kapleau, Philip. *The Three Pillars of Zen: Teaching, Practice, and Enlightenment.* New York: Anchor Books, 1989.

Reps, Paul, and Nyogen Senzaki. *Zen Flesh, Zen Bones: A Collection of Zen and Pre-Zen Writings.* Boston: Tuttle Publishing, 1998.

Shunryu, Suzuki. *Zen Mind, Beginner's Mind.* New York: Shambhala Publications, 2006.

Watts, Alan. *The Way of Zen.* New York: Vintage Books, 1957.

Yamada, Koun. *Zen: The Authentic Gate.* Somerville, MA: Wisdom Publications, 2015.

Mark Morse, trans. *The Gateless Gate: The Classic Book of Zen Koans.* Berkeley: Counterpoint, 2019.

Zen Training: Methods and Philosophy. By Katsuki Sekida. Boston: Shambhala Publications, 2005.